How Do Dinosaurs

Say I Love You?

TAPEJARA

NOTHOSAURUS

TSINTAOSAURUS

CAUDIPTERYX

PACHYCEPHALOSAURUS

NEOVENATOR

KENTROSAURUS

OURANOSAURUS

ANTARCTOSAURUS

CHASMOSAURUS

TAPEJARA

NOTHOSAURUS

TSINTAOSAURUS

CAUDIPTERYX

PACHYCEPHALOSAURUS

NEOVENATOR

KENTROSAURUS

OURANOSAURUS

ANTARCTOSAURUS

CHASMOSAURUS

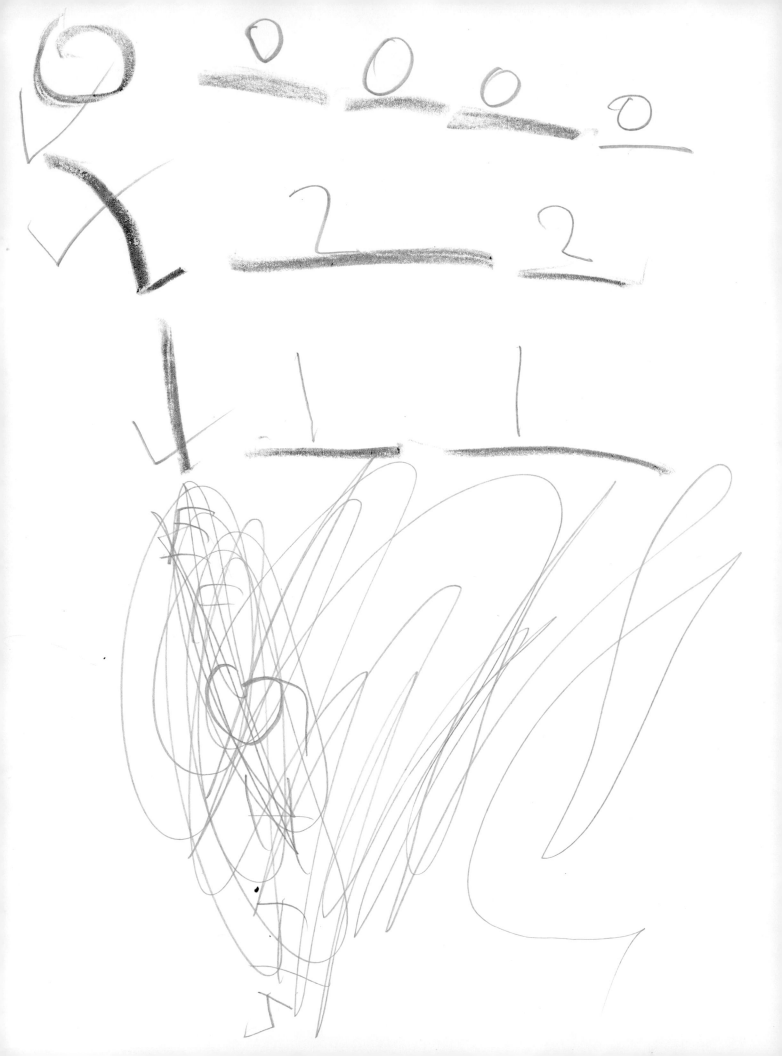

JANE YOLEN

How Do Dinosaurs

Say I Love You?

Illustrated by
MARK TEAGUE

SCHOLASTIC INC.
New York Toronto London Auckland
Sydney Mexico City New Delhi Hong Kong

This book was originally published in hardcover by The Blue Sky Press in 2009.

ISBN 978-0-545-33076-3

Text copyright © 2009 by Jane Yolen. Illustrations copyright © 2009 by Mark Teague.

All rights reserved. Published by Scholastic Inc. SCHOLASTIC and associated

logos are trademarks and/or registered trademarks of Scholastic Inc.

12 11 10 9 8 7 6 5 4 3 2 1   11 12 13 14 15 16/0

Printed in the U.S.A.   08

This edition first printing, January 2011

The artwork was created using acrylic paint.

Designed by Kathleen Westray

To wee dinosaur
David Stemple
J. Y.

To Mom
M. T.

You woke in the morning

in such a bad mood . . .

NEOVENATOR

then sat at the table
and fussed with
your food.

But then you blew kisses
and waved from the door.
I love you, I love you,
my dinosaur.

OURANOSAURUS

Out in the sandbox
you threw lots of sand.

CHASMOSAURUS

You ran from the slide,
after slapping
my hand.

But you suddenly turned
with a smile I adore.
Oh, I'll always
love you,
my dinosaur.

You moped through your nap time
and slept not a wink.

You flooded the house when you played in the sink.

But you got out the mop
and then cleaned
up the floor!
I love you
so much,
little dinosaur.

Off in the car,
you kept kicking
my seat . . .

and when we got out,
you were dragging
your feet.

But you held my hand tight
when we walked in the store.
I'll love you forever,
my dinosaur.

NOTHOSAURUS

Dinner disaster!

You made such a mess!

Would you stay up past bedtime?

The answer was

YES!

But when you smile sweetly
and hold back your roar,
when you kiss me and hug me
once, twice, even more . . .

. . . that's when you give love,
and I know this is true,
because *that's* how a dinosaur says
I Love You!

a b c d e f
f

t k k

h k
k

R B
S

x r k
o p q

k
2
E
f

TAPEJARA

NOTHOSAURUS

TSINTAOSAURUS

CAUDIPTERYX

PACHYCEPHALOSAURUS

NEOVENATOR

KENTROSAURUS

OURANOSAURUS

ANTARCTOSAURUS

CHASMOSAURUS

TAPEJARA

NOTHOSAURUS

TSINTAOSAURUS

CAUDIPTERYX

PACHYCEPHALOSAURUS

NEOVENATOR

KENTROSAURUS

OURANOSAURUS

ANTARCTOSAURUS

CHASMOSAURUS